DAMN VALENTINE

HALEY TRAVIS

DEDICATION

*This book is dedicated to the incredibly hard-working audio,
video, and show techs of North America, and their understanding
partners and families who deal with their mixed-up schedules
and perpetual lack of sleep.
Thank you for always ensuring the show goes on.*

1

* NIKKI *

I was determined to avoid meeting cute guys tonight. No matter what.

I'd never been so glammed up, sugar high, and slightly irritated. I told my friend Karen a thousand times that I would not be going out this New Year's Eve, for fear of repeating the pattern that happened to me for the past three years. I'd meet a guy, we'd date, he would think I was getting serious when I wasn't, and we'd crash and burn just before Valentine's Day.

No more. For this New Year's, I was going to stay in and watch the sparkling ball drop on TV from the comfort of my own couch.

But Karen whined and begged and pleaded for me to come to a New Year's party with her. The guy she had a massive crush on, who was obviously the perfect man for her and there were no others, was her friend Monica's brother. They were co-hosting the party so Karen absolutely had to go.

I really wanted to put my foot down, but Karen had been

so wonderful to me during my weird three to five week relationships every January that I had to do a favor for her.

"Who knows," she had said, "Maybe this year you'll meet a great guy."

"Not a chance," I replied grimly. My determination was palpable.

Yet here I was, getting all dolled up at Karen's condo while we ate an entire bowl full of candy and split a bottle of Moscato. Then an energy drink. I wasn't tipsy at all, I was sugar high. It felt like I'd had an entire pot of coffee by the time we left.

The party was just a few blocks away, which was perfect. I could have walked home if I decided to leave early, or I could go back to Karen's and crash at her place so that we could do a giant hangover breakfast.

She was weirdly excited to 'accidentally' run into Chris, this guy she had been drooling after in a most unladylike fashion. I found myself becoming swept up in her excitement. There's nothing like that feeling of butterflies at the start of a new relationship when everything is bright and full of possibility. The first three dates are usually magical. But that's when a few real conversations have to take place, and where things can start falling apart before they're even really started.

New Year's was supposed to be the time to break old habits and start new traditions. I was only twenty-five, and if it was going to happen again, this would be the fourth year of what I called 'the curse'.

Sure, the beginning of the year was a great time to meet new people when they were all riled up after the holidays, and wanting to start a fresh new year with a fresh new person. It was great, until the pressure of Valentine's Day loomed, and guys seemed to think that I was after something serious. I wasn't. I mean, eventually. But I would have been happy casually dating for a few months until we figured things out.

I was much better off staying single for a bit longer.

Karen was practically bouncing up and down by the time we got to Monica's condo. I don't even quite know how Karen knew her – a work connection or something. But she got a look at Monica's brother and pretty much lost her mind. Hey, everyone has a type.

As we went in, dropping off the obligatory hostess gift of a bottle of good red wine, and two bottles of cheap white that we were likely going to drink tonight, I noticed that it was already ten after eleven. Great, I thought to myself. I could make the rounds, chitchat, and leave by one am if I wasn't having a fabulous time.

There were at least forty people milling around, and everyone was quite open and chatty. For once it was relatively easy to start talking with strangers. Everyone was in a festive mood, which made the evening much easier for me, since I'm usually pretty shy.

I had a wonderful conversation with a gal about her hot pink boots. Then I was chatting with a slightly older gentleman about how the transit system in Toronto is falling apart, and nobody is listening because the people in charge never even take the subway.

I was careful to only drink one more small glass of wine so that I could keep my mission on point. No guys, no matter what. Just friendly conversation.

As the living room became packed and rowdy, I did a sweep for abandoned glasses, washing them quickly and leaving them in the rack to dry. I knew that hostesses always became overwhelmed, so I usually tried to spend five minutes helping them catch up, even if they never knew it was me.

The huge flat-screen lit up, and everyone gathered in the living room as glasses of champagne were handed out. It was three minutes until midnight, and I grinned to myself. This was it. The year the curse would be broken. This was the year I was going to take charge of my love life, and figure out what I truly wanted, even though I wasn't looking right now.

This was the year I was going to work on being a little less shy, a bit more outgoing, and take charge at the office. Since I was younger than many of the staff, I'd never really asserted myself. It was time for me to, for lack of a better term, find some balls. I almost laughed out loud to myself realizing that women truly needed a better term for being confident and self-assured.

Karen came running over, gripping my hand tightly and practically bouncing in her perfect chocolate brown designer outfit. "Chris and I were just talking for over twenty minutes, and I think he really likes me."

"That's great," I said, truly excited for my friend.

"Are you okay if I take off to stand right beside him for the countdown?"

"Go get him, girl," I grinned. Being alone was never something I had a problem with.

As she took off, I moved into the center of the crowd where I could be part of the group's excitement, yet ignored if necessary. Everyone here was smiling and friendly. Even though most of them were strangers, there was a very positive vibe.

I was so relieved to kick the energy of the previous years behind that I was actually smiling from ear to ear into my champagne glass. Who cares, I thought. Everyone was a bit tipsy. They won't remember seeing the weird girl practically giggling to herself.

The thought of shaking off the negative energy caused actual butterflies in the pit of my stomach. But then I felt something else. Jerking my head up, I looked into the most hypnotic dark blue eyes I'd ever seen.

"Ten..." everyone chanted.

The eyes came closer, carefully pushing through the crowd. He was tall, dark and handsome in a scruffy, rough sort of way.

"Nine..." everyone hollered.

He stopped directly in front of me.

"Eight..."

He was staring at me with the strangest expression, and I felt my spine begin to twitch.

"Seven..."

He was huge, with broad, muscled shoulders barely concealed in a tight black t-shirt. I felt absolutely tiny next to him.

"Six..."

He slid an arm around me, slowly pulling me against his hard, warm body.

"Five..."

The draw toward him was unearthly. Magnetic. My eyes were wide, but I wasn't afraid. Just curious.

"Four..."

Lowering his lips to my ear, he whispered, "May I kiss you?" His voice was so low, enticing.

"Three..."

I looked up at him, nodding as he smiled sweetly.

"Two..."

Like lightning, he set my glass down on the table behind me and wrapped one arm around my lower back, the other around my shoulders, with his hand stretched upward to cradle the back of my head as he tipped my mouth up to his.

"One..."

His lips met mine a second early, stopping my breath and causing my heart to race like a jackrabbit.

People screamed and cheered all around us, but all I could hear was my pulse in my ears and a soft low moan that may have been me.

His tender kiss drew heat from both of us, building to an enchanting burn that I felt down my back and through my hips. Winding my hands in the back of his thick black hair, I felt his lips part slightly, inviting me in.

Tentatively, I allowed the tip of my tongue to creep along his bottom lip, entering his mouth slowly. I swear I felt him shudder in my arms as he grazed his tongue against mine. His strong arms pulled us closer until we were entwined almost indecently. It didn't matter since we were the only two people in the world.

This time I was pretty sure the next little moan was his, as I felt him curling around me, drawing me against his body so tightly it felt like he wanted to swallow me whole. His lower hand slid down to gently cup my ass, and I felt a wave of lust that was like a physical shock flashing through me.

My entire body was pressed to his, and I've never needed a man this desperately before. His tongue cradled mine, dancing and exploring as we rocked together in overpowering bliss.

Reluctantly, he pulled back, gazing gently into my eyes as if searching for something. "I'm sorry," he said in a gravelly, low tone. "I don't know what the hell just came over me."

"That's okay," I said with an embarrassed little smile. "Um, I'm Nikki."

"Alex," he said, leaning back in to kiss along the top of my cheekbone. I'd never been held by a guy this huge before, and feeling like a tiny doll in his arms was overwhelming.

He released me quickly, giving his head a shake as if the magical spell were broken, then took off into the kitchen, where I saw him talking quickly and seriously to Chris. I was left feeling empty. Hollow. Taking a deep breath, I tried to clear the strange aftershocks.

Then a hand took mine, and I looked up as Alex dragged me out of the living room and down the hallway to where it was quieter.

Backing me up against the wall, his kiss was wild. Primal. Feeling his hot, hard body pressed against me was so sensual that I couldn't catch my breath again.

"I'm so sorry, gorgeous," he murmured in my ear. "I have to leave five minutes ago."

Then his hands gripped my hips hard as his mouth nearly devoured me. I heard a buzz from a vibrating phone. "Damn," he growled, pulling away, and releasing me. Staring into my eyes for just a second, he grinned. "I'll call you, Nikki."

He vanished out the front door before I'd even caught my breath. Slowly walking out to the living room again, I felt like I was floating.

Karen appeared out of nowhere. "What the hell was that?" she asked, laughing her head off.

"I have no idea."

"Who was that guy?"

"I have no idea."

She looked at me with her mouth hanging open for a

solid three seconds. "You little skank," she teased, as only a best friend could.

I tried to compose myself and focus. "Did you get that New Year's kiss from Chris?"

"Not really," she said. "Well, sort of. There was a circle of five people, each giving everyone a tiny peck. So it was a start, I guess." She grinned again. "Not at all like what I saw happening over here." I reached down to pick up my champagne glass, chugging the entire thing.

Strangely, I felt amazing. Like everything in my world was brighter. Luckily, Karen grabbed my hand and pulled me over to where we could dance off the sugar high for an hour.

2

* ALEX *

I've never done such a crazy thing before in my life. Racing toward that gorgeous girl, grabbing her and kissing her the way I did... It was completely unlike me. If I had seen another guy do that, I would have been concerned for the poor girl. But I had waited for her to nod. She had certainly said yes with her eyes.

Then she definitely said yes with the rest of her body. I will never forget the feeling of her delicate little fingers caressing the back of my neck. The taste of her silky lips will haunt me forever.

Part of me can't quite believe I didn't haul her away to the bedroom immediately.

Having that sort of a reaction to a woman was not normal for me. Sure, I liked girls, and dated now and then, but this was different. It was as if the universe itself had tapped me on the shoulder and said, "Hey buddy – there's your girl."

It was devastating to have to run off on her, but I had to get back to work. I'd only dropped by because Chris needed some important files for a project he was working on, and I happened to be working a gig three blocks away. After I handed him the USB keys, I tried to leave immediately, but Nikki's face caught my eye, then my heart.

The next day I waited until the afternoon to send Chris a text, not wanting to wake him up if he happened to have a New Year's hangover.

Hey – I need the full name and number of a girl who was at your party last night. Nikki. Short light blonde hair, big blue eyes. Sort of short, with full, hourglass curves.

I had to wait almost an hour for a response.

Sorry, I don't know her. My sister Monica had a bunch of friends over as well. I'll ask her.

I felt a strange creeping darkness crawl through the pit of my stomach. There was no way I could have found the girl of my dreams and then lost her.

Hey – Monica doesn't know her either. She recalls a girl like that dropping by with another of her friends, but can't remember her name. She blames the champagne. Sorry.

Damn. I set my phone carefully on my coffee table so that I wouldn't hurl it against the wall. Maybe in a couple of days, Monica would remember. I'm sure I could find her through Chris on social media. That would mean hours of checking through friends of friends. Or, maybe I'll just wait a few days until all of the New Year's photos were posted, and I could find her there.

There was no way I was going to lose this girl. Even though I had to quickly pack my gear bags and get ready to haul ass to the airport for another job.

3

———

*** NIKKI ***

I spent the entire next day searching for Alex online, but I didn't have any leads beyond seeing him speaking with Chris in the kitchen. I quickly confirmed online that it had been Karen's big crush, but he had no friends named Alex on any social media page.

My mind raced. I wasn't going to give up. Why would someone drop into a party for three minutes? Alex had said he had to be somewhere in a hurry. What if he wasn't a friend, he was a coworker?

I checked out the company Chris apparently worked for, and found out that his office was not too far from mine.

Feeling like a crazy stalker, I spent every lunch hour, and an hour after work, sitting in the window of the coffee shop directly beside the doors of the office tower, trying to casually read a book. I rarely deviated from my usual schedule, so I tried to tell myself that this was a learning experience.

I felt ridiculous, but the thought of never seeing Alex again was too much to bear. Just three work days. That was a reasonable amount of time to be hopeful without being completely nuts. Or at least, that's what I told myself.

But at the end of the third evening, I watched as the clock passed six. Then six-ten. At six-twenty, I slipped my book into my purse, threw out my coffee cup, and left the cafe feeling completely dejected.

"Thank god I found you, Nikki." The voice was so low. Nearly a growl.

I spun to look up into Alex's eyes. There was something so sensual about him. It was almost unnerving, but I could feel his heat through my bones just from him standing so close to me.

"I'm so sorry I took off on New Year's. I was trying to get your number from Chris because... There's just something about you." His deep eyes locked on mine with an intensity that was nearly paralyzing. "Nikki, I can't stop thinking about that kiss."

Alex leaned in cautiously, as if checking to see if I'd pull away. But I couldn't. His lips on mine were so soft, as if he was testing my response. I nearly whimpered with instant desire, as our arms snaked around each other.

He pulled me off the sidewalk into a little nook between buildings. Part of me couldn't believe that I was openly making out with this guy in public. Part of me couldn't believe that I'd found him again. But most of me was simply melting, as he held me to the wall, pressing his body against mine.

Unzipping my coat, he opened it so that he could run his hands around my waist. Somehow he untucked my shirt, sliding his hands up my back. A cloud of raw lust had overtaken me, dulling basic functions like common sense and decency.

His lips left mine to glide down my throat. "Nikki, baby," he murmured, "I can't let you go again. I can't. But I have to leave town for a few days for work. I'm running home to pack right now." He nuzzled my ear, whispering, "Can I see you as soon as I'm back?"

I nodded, my fingers clenched into the back of his hair. He smelled incredible. Earthy. His flashing eyes were so intense. I felt like I was under a spell.

An alarm of some kind went off on his phone, and he groaned. He stroked my back another moment, whispering, "You're so soft," into my ear, his breath warm and intimate.

Then he straightened up, digging out his phone and hitting some buttons. "Hey – give me your phone?" I handed it to him instantly.

He opened the camera and held it out, placing his lips to my cheek as he took a selfie of the two of us, with me giggling. His fingers flew over the surface of the phone for a moment, setting something up. Then I heard his phone beep.

"I've set myself up as one of your contacts so that I can text you and let you know when I'll be back."

"Okay." I suddenly felt lost.

Alex cocked his head, looking at me oddly. Then his eyes flew wide. "I'm so sorry, Nikki. I know I'm really forward, and a bit loud. You're a shy little thing, aren't you?"

I nodded. "Sometimes."

"Don't worry, we'll balance each other out," he grinned. "Quick – tell me something fun you're going to do while I'm gone."

"Um, I have a lot of knitting to catch up on."

"Cool," he smiled. "Artsy crafty. I'll see you in a few days."

His mouth glided across mine in a kiss so deep I felt it in my hips. Then his lips tapped my forehead. "I'll miss you," he said softly, staring into my eyes for longer than I would normally have been comfortable with. Then he was gone.

Leaning against the wall, I zipped up my coat, wondering what the hell just happened. Lifting my phone, I saw that he'd entered his number as a contact labeled, "Alex 'the man in my life' Danby", with the photo he took of us as the icon.

He'd also sent a text to himself as if it were from me. "Alex, this is Nikki. I know that I am the prettiest girl you've ever seen, but I'm also interesting, and I'm going to tell you all about myself when we have dinner in a few days." I laughed all the way home.

For the next three days, I found myself bursting into smiles and laughter for no apparent reason. Alex was too forward, too outgoing for me. Yet he was right – maybe we would balance each other out?

The first day he was gone, he sent me a photo of a huge pile of cables that were tangled across the floor of what looked like a huge corporate event space. "I hope you're having a better day than mine, gorgeous. But I'm thinking of you, and that makes everything better.

I sent him a photo of my desk at work, with everything laid out perfectly at right angles, with brightly colored markers on top of my notebook. "The queen of organization is displeased by that cable arrangement. I hope it works out. The markers and I believe in you."

The next day around noon he sent a photo of a giant coffee mug, with just his eyes peering over it. "This photo was taken at three am. I wish that I could sleep so that I could dream of you. But that seems unlikely."

I replied with a photo of myself holding up a teacup with my pinky finger extended, tilting my head so that only one eye was in frame. "Pinkies up means time for tea. Sorry that you're not getting much sleep."

The third day he sent a photo of a huge old fashioned

clock in what looked like a hotel lobby. "Counting the minutes until I can see you. What's your address, and can I come over as soon as my flight gets in tomorrow night around five?"

I sent my address, and immediately began planning dinner. I texted, "Any food allergies or restrictions?"

He replied immediately. "I eat everything. Please don't go to any trouble. I could order something. I'll likely arrive around six. Warning – I'm going to hug you to pieces."

I'd never looked forward to a date this much in my life. Since Alex had likely been eating hotel and restaurant food for the past few days, I made a spinach and mandarin orange salad, and spiral pasta with beef and yellow peppers.

I found a dark blue dress that nearly matched his eyes, and flowed over my generous hips in a casually sexy way. I hoped that he didn't think I was leading him on, as this would not be a booty call. But we hadn't really talked much yet.

Curiosity was spiraling through my mind. Was he looking for a real relationship? Did he just want a fling?

My phone beeped with a text at five-forty-three. "Flight was a bit late. In a cab on my way to you right now."

Opening the door of my apartment two seconds after he knocked, he barreled in, rolling a suitcase behind him. He dragged it inside, dropping his shoulder bag, shutting the door behind him before gathering me in his arms.

"Look at you, gorgeous," he breathed. Then he was already kissing me. He kicked off his shoes, pulling me to the couch, pulling me on top of him as he laid down. His hands caressed me firmly through my dress, his mouth devouring mine.

It was amazing getting to know someone purely through

the feeling of desire. I knew that there would be more, but for now, it was all I could think of.

I was relieved that he didn't go further, just kissing me for at least ten minutes before sitting up and pulling me into his lap. "Dinner smells amazing, baby, but I was starving for you."

My giggle surprised me. "Where were you?"

"Oh – damn. Sorry I didn't mention it. I was at a gig in Vancouver."

"What do you do? And why were the cables such a mess?"

He grinned. "I'm a supervisor and tech for an audio-video company that works corporate gigs. We were running microphones through a sound system that I'm pretty sure has been around since dinosaurs walked the earth." His rumbling chuckle shook my shoulder.

"What sort of gig?"

"It was an annual meeting of some financial company. A bunch of guys in suits talking about how great they all were this year, and how great they think they'll be next year." His fingers wandered into the back of my hair. "What do you do? Your desk looked very official."

"I'm the office manager and coordinator at an educational book production company."

"And your markers and fancy office supplies keep you company?"

"Yeah. I need someone to have deep conversations with now and then."

"I'm here now," he said softly. "I work weird hours, and my sleep schedule is completely messed up, but you can always text me, or leave me voicemail anytime. Okay?"

"Oh. Okay."

He bounced me on his knee, staring into my eyes. "I was

working a gig New Year's eve. Split shift, I had to race back to the show. I thought that Chris would have your name and number so that I could get in touch after, but he didn't know you."

"I was there with my friend Karen who was a friend of his sister, Monica."

Alex shook his head. "Dammit. I'm so sorry, Nikki." He squeezed me tightly. "You're stuck with me now though." Then he tipped my chin up with his finger. "Is that okay? You don't have a truckload of men that you're currently dating?"

I giggled again, shaking my head. "Not that I'm aware of."

"And is it okay if I shuffle in here and announce that I'm your boyfriend now? Because that's what's happening."

The second I began to nod, he kissed me again, gripping the back of my hair gently as he pulled me to him.

4

* ALEX *

After an incredibly delicious dinner, chatting about our jobs and everything under the sun, I realized I'd never been this possessive or direct with a woman before. It wasn't me, even as I led her back to the couch to cuddle her on my lap again. I had no idea why this was happening. But everything about Nikki caused alarms to ring in the back of my mind, screaming that she was the one.

The problem was, my life wasn't set up to be good for relationships. Uptight women would be driven nuts in days. My schedule was never my own, and women always seemed to be offended that I couldn't drop a three-day job to meet their friends or take them shopping.

My life and my work were thoroughly weird sometimes, and I could only be with a girl if she was okay rolling with it. I didn't do one night stands, or two-week flings, which is what many of my coworkers tended to gravitate to. I just couldn't do it. But I also couldn't make promises that I wasn't sure that I could keep.

Every time I was invited to an event, I had to respond, "Probably, if I'm not working."

The other thing that women had to understand about me was that my schedule was insane. Not just busy, although working sixteen-hour shifts was certainly part of it. Days might go by when I was asleep whenever she was awake. I could always text, but sometimes the timing didn't line up for phone calls.

I needed a woman who had her own life to entertain her when I wasn't around. There was no way I could be in one of those couples where they were inseparable and did everything together.

Nikki seemed to have a few things going on. Work, friends, and her knitting, likely more. I'm positive she also read a lot. It seemed like she might be the kind of girl who would be okay with just a date or two per week during the busy season.

I hoped that she wasn't too clingy. My instinctive male reaction was to want to care for her, but I couldn't always be there in person. Was she really the girl who would click with me, and get it?

So far she had seemed completely chill. Everything about her was fascinating and adorable. I couldn't wait to know more about her. I just hoped that I could hold my physical urges in check for a while. It had been a long time since I'd been with a woman, and Nikki was so sexy it was hard not to drag her to the bedroom right this second. Very, very hard.

Pulling her into my arms on the couch, the way her lips clung to mine was driving me wild. Every kiss was sweeter than the last, and her soft little gasps sent shudders straight through me.

Running my hands along her back, holding her against

me, it was difficult to control myself. But I couldn't frighten her away. She seemed a little nervous. I knew that I was too forward most of the time, so I pulled away.

"You're delicious, sweet little Nikki," I murmured. "Thank you for dinner."

"You're welcome," she beamed. "I'm glad you liked it. I'm not much of a cook."

"I think you are." My lips trailed along her cheekbone. "But for dessert, I want this little bit right here." Bringing my mouth to her throat just under her ear, she gasped as I kissed her, trembling in my arms.

From the way her breathing sounded so tight and rattled, I realized she really was nervous. Maybe she didn't have a lot of experience with men.

"Baby, someday I might be pushy and invite myself over, but I can't stay tonight," I murmured against her neck. Sitting up straighter, I kissed her forehead. "I have about ten hours to do laundry, sleep, and get back to the airport. I'm leaving early."

Her pretty eyes flew wide. "I... why did you waste your time coming here at all?"

Running my thumb along her bottom lip, I grinned. "I was hungry for this kiss." As my lips met hers again, the fire between us was unmistakable. I knew she wanted me, she just wasn't quite ready yet. That was fine. I would never pressure her. But I did want to give her a preview of what was definitely to come.

Pulling her against me suddenly, her breathless gasp was unbelievably sexy. "You're more delicious than dinner," I growled into her lips. "And your little moans drive me wild, baby."

She blushed, as I kissed across her warm cheeks.

"Listen," I said gently, "This next job is a really tricky

show, and I might be super distracted, and not answer your messages right away. But it would make me very happy if you could text me and let me know how your day is going, okay? Tell me everything."

She nodded. "Okay. But I don't want to bother you."

"Never. My phone is on silent during shows, or when I really need to sleep. So text as much as you like." I kissed her suddenly again, hot and deep until she moaned. "And send me a photo of yourself now and then so I don't get lonely."

Her precious grin lit up my heart. "Okay."

I hated having to let go of her and stand up, but I really did have to wash my work clothes before my flight.

Kissing her once more at the door, I said, "I'll be back in five days. Wait – six? Sorry, I'll let you know. I'm so tired I don't even know what day it is."

Her eyes tightened with concern. "Get some sleep and I hope your job goes well." Then she grinned. "No more piles of tangled cables."

I rolled my eyes. "Let's hope."

I nuzzled her ear once more, whispering, "You're gorgeous, baby. I'm so glad I found you."

Nikki's sweet smile as she closed the door gave me the strength to make it home, nearly dead on my feet.

5

* NIKKI *

All night long I had strange, vivid dreams about Alex. It was far too soon for him to be acting like we were a couple. Wasn't it? Since none of my previous attempts at dating had worked out, maybe I should try to go with the flow.

The problem was, I rarely flowed. I was, as Karen reminded me frequently, a bit uptight. Most of my life was on a schedule, except for the times where I had an evening booked off to go out with her, knowing that she'd be in charge of timing for the whole night.

Karen thought that I was far too tightly wound. But the truth was, I was sometimes hit with waves of shyness and anxiety. It normally wasn't too bad, but the thing that helped me control it was knowing what was happening. I knew that I had to survive the workday until five, the streetcar until five-forty, then I had a calming list of activities and chores until bedtime.

I knew that sounded completely boring, and I was fine altering my schedule when I needed to. Yet knowing when things were going to unfold gave me a sense of control in a busy city that often had too many things happening at once.

When the time was carved into bite-sized chunks, I knew how to behave. How to manage my energy.

I knew that was why Karen had dragged me to the New Year's party in the first place. She wanted to help me become more accustomed to chatting with strangers.

I truly appreciated her help and concern. Over the years, she'd helped with my glitches quite a bit. I'd returned the favor by helping the chaos of her unstructured life by helping her to develop a few routines and systems. It took two years, but I finally got her onto a day planner and to-do list style that she actually used.

The thing with a good friend is that we were both just the right amount of pushy, in a healthy, caring way. I'd always wondered what a romantic relationship like that would be. My first two attempts at dating were with men who could only be described as wishy-washy. Perhaps rudderless. They were cute slackers who stumbled through life getting by on their smiles. I couldn't handle that complete lack of direction.

The third guy was so regimented and driven that it was impossible to become part of his life. He had four hours open on Saturday nights for a date, and that was it. When I suggested keeping in touch through the week, he gave me a pitying look as if I were some sort of clingy monster. So that was the end of that.

I knew that this might seem like a bit of a 'Goldilocks' situation, but I wanted a guy who was just right. Who I could spend a reasonable amount of time with, but who would also check in with me daily, just so that we could stay close.

The entire next day, I powered through a huge workload

while trying to figure out what sort of text would make Alex grin while he was working in... where did he say he was? He didn't.

My job as an office manager for an educational book production company was absolutely perfect for me. The rest of the employees were mostly mellow. Everyone was fine with most of our communication happening through email.

I processed the written word with much more efficiency, so this allowed me to be quick and accurate. Creating schedules, managing workloads, and coordinating teams for each project based both on their skills and their strengths was something I was truly good at.

Some days I felt like an air traffic controller as the people and projects flowed around quickly under my direction. But today, every time I looked down at my to-do list, I saw a tiny extra dot in the margin. That was my reminder to think about what to say to Alex.

Finally, at quarter to four, I sent him a text.

Hi! I hope your gig is going well. My day was pretty good – I put together two work teams, coordinated three projects, and had a fabulous chicken Caesar salad from a new place around the corner. Not exciting, but a nice day. Where are you again? I hope that everything is going your way today.

I hoped that chatty and casual was the right tone. This habit of second guessing myself at every possible opportunity had to stop. Other people just ran around living their lives. They didn't run through every conversation three times before opening their mouths.

Alex's impulsiveness in both taking hold of me and kissing me, and inviting himself to my place to tell me that he was now my boyfriend, were both confident moves. Direct. There was something about that sort of forthright energy that inspired me. As much as I wanted to be with him, I also secretly wished that I could be just a little more like him.

When I got home and began making dinner, I got a text from Alex.

Hey there, baby. Glad you had a good day. Salad is always the best lunch. Not exciting, but good brain fuel. Your friend says hello.

The next message was a photo of Alex's eye looking at a little duck magnet that he was holding up, with the airport sign "Welcome to Calgary" in the background.

My eyes darted to the fridge. I hadn't noticed that my duck was missing. Bursting out laughing, I fell on the couch, my fingers twitching as I typed.

Kidnapper! No, ducknapper! I hadn't even noticed that he was gone. I hope that the two of you have a nice time.

I couldn't believe how completely adorable he was to actually take something of mine on his trip with him. It made me feel immediately closer to him. He was thinking about me even when I wasn't with him.

With other guys, I felt like I disappeared from their world the second I was out of sight. Like our relationship only existed when we were in the same room. For Alex to plan ahead to amuse me... The grin I wore was stretching my face.

6

*** ALEX ***

I was glad that Nikki seemed okay with my ducknapping. I had been looking everywhere around her apartment for something I could take that wasn't valuable, and likely didn't have great sentimental value, just in case it got lost on my trip.

It was important for me to show her that she was part of my world now, even when communication was sporadic.

The job today had been an entirely new dimension of exhausting, with tech glitches, broken gear, and a fussy client that kept trying to help by getting in our way. But as always, things were sorted out and perfectly smooth fifteen minutes before show time.

Running on adrenaline and cheap hotel coffee was really no way to live, and there were times when I felt like I was floating around in a haze. By the time I finally got to my hotel room, I was ready to collapse, knowing that I'd have a twelve-hour day tomorrow, starting at unreasonable hours of the morning.

Jumping in the shower, I felt a little brighter when I got back to the bed to attend to the sandwiches I'd liberated from the buffet around lunch. I was too tired to bother going out for dinner.

Placing the duck on my pillow, with my face beside it, I took an awkward selfie of me smiling up to the phone. Checking the time difference, Nikki was likely going to bed around now.

Duckie and I are hoping that you have sweet dreams tonight.

About ten minutes later, I received a photo of Nikki with her head on the pillow, wearing a light blue sleep mask that read, "Sweet Dreams". Her light blonde hair was fanned around her in a little halo, and those plush pink lips taunted me.

I sent her one more message.

Gorgeous. XOX

Turning the phone off, I ate quickly so that I could get a solid six hours of sleep. I was dying to call her, but knew that I wouldn't be at my best if I didn't get a certain amount of sleep. And I knew that once I got chatting to the new pretty little sweetheart in my life, I'd never let her hang up.

7

My stomach was fluttering from Alex's goodnight messages all day long. I'd never really texted a guy very much before, and never sent photos as communication. I saw my phone as a utility device. Something I used to ask for directions or to inform someone I was running late because the subways were backed up.

I guess Alex used it as much more of a real communication tool to stay in touch. I wondered how much he was on the road. He said this was a busy season, but living this way all year long was a strange concept. Perhaps this was one of those things that were thrown in my path to teach me lessons. To show me that being so uptight wasn't healthy and that I should chill out. It was something that I'd been meaning to try.

Paperwork and scheduling flew past me and through me during the hectic start of the day. I wondered if there was something that I could do that would perk up my team. Everyone had been working very hard, and I knew that we'd be hit with a major influx of work in a week or two. Perhaps conserving energy and improving morale was a good thing to do before we needed it. I noticed that today's workload was more than reasonable.

Like a turtle growing to fit its aquarium, the workload tended to fill whatever space it had. People would take their time if they had all day, but would pick up the pace and get things done quickly if they had to.

My boss, Matt, had gently encouraged me a few times to take the reigns and do whatever I thought was needed for the good of the team. Was I bold enough to try something a bit crazy?

After weighing the pros and cons for a few minutes, I thought of my New Year's resolution to be a bit bolder. Then I thought of Alex, heading straight for me, and basically claiming me as his from one glance. If he could do that, I could do one odd little thing for the good of my coworkers.

At eleven in the morning, I sent out an all-hands email, asking if it was possible for everyone to clear all projects by three pm so that we could have an important team meeting from then to the end of the day.

Nobody questioned why. Most of them likely assumed that I would be dropping a work bomb on them for the weekend. But there were no complaints. Everyone was assembled in the large meeting room by three-twenty-nine, and my boss looked at me expectantly.

Clearing my throat slightly, I tried to speak up a bit. "As you all know, we tend to get a ton of emergency projects dumped on us at the end of January, and we'll all end up working late several times."

Everyone shrugged, nodding.

"So, it's Friday. We're caught up. Let's go home early." Glancing at Matt, he stared at me, incredulous.

Then he chuckled. "All right folks, you heard Nikki. Everyone get lost!"

There was a brief pause as everyone realized that this wasn't some sort of joke. Then a round of laughter filled the room, along with a chorus of, "Thanks, Nikki," and "Have a great weekend."

Matt clapped me on the shoulder. "Great idea, Nikki. Reward everyone before the busy spell. Good work."

The streetcar home wasn't jammed. The grocery store wasn't packed. It was amazing what an hour and a half difference made.

I had disrupted the schedules for an entire office full of twelve people, and everyone was happy about it. The one person I needed to tell immediately was Alex.

Today I was a giant liar. I pulled the whole office into a "meeting" at 3:30 then sent them home early. For a few minutes, I felt like a hero. That was weird, and nice. I hope you're having a great day.

He replied in about an hour.

Baby, I'm so proud of you! You're a superstar. My day is adequate. Busy, slow, but everything is working. I can't wait to hold you in my arms in a few days.

The thought of his arms around me instantly made me melt. It was strange that I didn't even know when he'd be back, or for how long. It was very strange that I hadn't asked him.

I didn't want to beg for too much information. I didn't want to seem fussy. Maybe I only wanted him to see a slightly less tightly wound version of myself.

8

---

* ALEX *

After sending Nikki a photo of her duck sitting on top of the soundboard, I packed up the essential gear and headed back to my room to crash. I realized that I didn't even know much about what she did for a living. I didn't know nearly enough about her hobbies and interests.

Rushing to an amazing Japanese place I always came to at least once while I was here, I picked up some vegetable-laden ramen to go. I hurried back to my room to take a quick shower, then had a few spoonfuls of dinner before calling Nikki quick before it got too late.

"Hello?" she answered softly.

"I'm sorry, did I wake you up?"

"No, I was just getting ready for bed."

"Good. So, you're a little sneak, letting your employees out early? You must realize that's not usually the way business people do their business stuff."

Her bright little laugh made me grin. "We're always slammed at the end of January, and have to work late sometimes. So I suddenly thought, since it's a slow day, why not make it up to them in advance?"

"You can just do that? You're the one in charge?"

"Well, no," she said quickly. "But my boss was really happy about it."

"You didn't ask permission first?"

She paused. "No. I knew he didn't know that it was slow, so, I just sort of did it."

"I'm so proud of you," I said, hoping that she could hear my grin. "That's amazing. What are you doing this weekend?"

I was learning that Nikki took her time speaking, which implied she thought first. I admired that.

"My knitting group meets every other Saturday afternoon."

"You make sweaters and things?"

Her soft laugh made me smile. "I'm not that great at complicated patterns yet. Some of the women do, though. Most of us just make hats, scarves, and mittens."

"Do you sell them?" I asked.

"No, we all pick up discount yarn whenever there's a sale, and we make warm things for the homeless."

"Wow, Nikki, that's so sweet of you."

"It's also a fun time," she said quickly. "We drink tea and talk about books and movies. It's a nice girly sort of afternoon."

"But you're spending your time doing something to keep strangers warm. I think that's amazing."

This time her pause felt more like she was trying to change the subject. "Thanks. How was your day?" she asked.

"If you hear slurping, I'm sorry, I'm eating ramen." She laughed, sounding like she was right here with me. "My day was busy but no challenges," I said.

"Is that good?"

"Most of the time, yes. Once in a while, it's exciting to have a challenge. Something interesting to solve, like a puzzle. I seem to be pretty good at that, and it's one of the reasons they have me run the crew most of the time. But challenges are only interesting on setup days, never during the show. That gets dangerous."

"Yeah, I could see that," she said.

"Is today Friday?" I asked.

She paused. "Yes. Are you serious?"

"I have the phone wedged under my ear so I can't see the calendar," I said. "Things get fuzzy when I'm on the road. I think we tear down after tomorrow's show, then fly back midday Sunday. I think. Probably."

Her sweet little laugh was even more delicious than the ramen. "That's crazy to not know your schedule."

"My phone knows it. I always know what's going on today, and one day ahead. Sometimes even two."

"Wow," she said softly. "How do you live like that?"

"I know. It's weird. But I check often to stay ahead of things. Well, most things." I chuckled. "Do feel free to remind me a lot if anything important is ever coming up."

"I'll try," she giggled. She paused for just a second, before practically whispering, "I hope I can see you soon."

"I can't wait to see you, baby. I'll text you when I'm on my way home, okay?"

"Okay."

"It's late in Toronto. You get to sleep. Sweet dreams. I miss you."

"I miss you too," she said softly. "Goodnight."

As I hung up and dove back into my dinner, I hoped that my schedule didn't freak her out too much. I knew that some women were super into schedules and lists and knowing what was up.

I would try harder to keep her informed. Stay connected with her. I had a great feeling about this sweet, gorgeous girl. This time, I was going to use a lot more of my scant amounts of extra energy to keep a closeness between us.

9

———

*** NIKKI ***

I was so looking forward to maybe seeing Alex on Sunday night that the rest of the weekend was a blur. Cleaning my apartment, knitting with the ladies for a few hours, dropping by the veggie market, picking up a new plant for the living room. My Saturdays were usually filled with homey things, but this time I was hoping that I'd have company to share it with.

Sunday afternoon just after one, a text came in.

Hey, baby. Just getting on the plane now. Pack up and load-out took twice as long due to the hotel staff being completely anal retentive about the elevators. Running on two hours of sleep. Hoping to sleep on the plane, but I need to go straight home for real sleep. Dead on feet. I will call you tomorrow. I think that's Monday?

As much as I was disappointed, I appreciated that he kept me posted.

Poor thing. I hope that you can nap on the plane, to be properly prepared for a big sleep. Yes, tomorrow is Monday, all day long. Take care of yourself, and I'll see you sometime soon.

I've never been good at switching gears, so perhaps this was good for me. Making myself a simple dinner, with leftovers packed for lunch the next day, I went over my weekly schedule before settling in for a movie.

All night long, I dreamed of Alex. As soon as our schedules aligned, I hoped that we'd really connect. Even though we hadn't spent much physical time together, I was feeling closer to him than I expected. Perhaps missing him was making him more desirable, on some weird subconscious level that I didn't understand.

Monday's workday came and went in a flurry of busyness. Several coworkers commented on how convenient Friday's early departure was, allowing them to catch up on things before their spouses and kids came home. It was amazing what a free hour could do. Maybe we were all too tightly scheduled.

We were all excited for our casual after-work event that night for Tim's birthday. He was the head of the graphic design department, so it was a tradition that we went out for a drink together. It was good to blow off a little steam and have some good conversations outside of the office.

By the time we were all crowded around four hastily pulled together tables on the top floor of a nearby pub, one drink turned into two at lightning speed.

I checked my phone around six, and there was a text from Alex.

I slept! I laundered! I am back to the land of the living, I think. How are you?

I responded immediately.

I am out having coworker birthday drinks at the Emperor's Library. I should be done by seven or so. What are you up to?

Tucking my phone away, I sank into a conversation with Thea about current design trends, especially those that were completely insane. Our laughter became louder, as others joined in.

Tim was getting a bit rowdy, in his silly amusing way, as he always did on everyone's birthday, but especially his. He came over to hug me from behind in my chair. "Thanks again for the early Friday, Nikki. So glad that we have you to keep us in line."

I grinned up at him, then turned back to Thea, to see Alex standing behind her.

"Oh my god!" I jumped up and bolted into his arms, not even thinking that my coworkers were staring.

He held me tight, murmuring into my hair. "I missed you so much, Nikki."

I quickly introduced him to everyone, and he seemed extremely concerned about making a good impression. But I let him know that I wanted to leave immediately by giving his hand a squeeze and nodding my head toward the door. I said my goodbyes, and then in minutes we were on the streetcar to my place.

"I didn't realize you were just going to show up," I giggled as he wrapped an arm around me.

"Surprise," he grinned. Then his eyes became cloudy. "Do you always hug your coworkers like that?"

I turned to hold his face in my hands. "Only on their birthdays. Maybe a few other special occasions." I felt myself biting my lip and stopped immediately. "You weren't jealous, were you?"

He took my hands in his, turning toward me on the seat. "I really was. I've never been jealous before. Honestly, I was completely shocked."

We got off the streetcar, and Alex spun me into his arms, kissing me so hard I nearly lost my breath. When he finally pulled away, his gorgeous smile glowed under the streetlight.

"Nikki, maybe I've never cared about a girl enough to feel jealous. Or possessive. I'm feeling all sorts of things that are brand new. But I think that's a good sign, right?"

I noted, stretching up to kiss him again. "I guess it's a good sign, as long as you understand I am going to hug people now and then. I'm a huggy person with people I've known for a long time."

Alex nodded. "I don't want you to change for me, Nikki. I'm just trying to sort through this weird instant connection."

I nodded, as we headed down the street. Alex immediately walked over to a homeless man sitting on the step of a convenience store. "Hey," he said, pulling a handful of slim packages from his shoulder bag. "Would you like some granola bars?"

The older man's face completely lit up as he took them. "Thanks, God bless you, man!"

Alex grinned, then took my hand as we turned onto the side street where my apartment was.

"That was really nice of you," I said.

"You inspired me, with your knitting hats. I'm always at events with free food in the hotels and the big conferences. Everybody loads up on those fancy granola bars. I might as well repurpose a few and get them to people who really need them."

"You're so sweet," I said, looking up at him as he returned my smile.

We walked quickly to my apartment, gravitating immediately to the couch. Before I even knew what was happening, Alex had pulled me into his lap, and we were softly caressing each other everywhere. I'd never been so aware of every single inch of my flesh.

My lips parted for his tongue, the scratch of his beard across my skin. I could never have even imagined a kiss like this. My entire nervous system was tingling, a strange current humming through me. I felt like I was floating, as his large hand untucked the back of my shirt to slip his palm up my back.

His lips slid down my neck, and I couldn't believe how sensitive my collarbone was as he nibbled along it.

"I've dreamed of this," Alex murmured. "When I was away, I was less lonely thinking of you, thinking of this moment."

I've never had a man seem so hungry for me, and it was making me tingle absolutely everywhere. Then I realized a certain part of my anatomy was reacting extremely strongly, which immediately made me nervous.

"You're making me crazy, Nikki," Alex groaned, wandering his open mouth back up my throat to capture my lips, kissing me so hard I was almost dizzy.

My hands explored his chest, his shoulders, then before I even realized I was doing it, I unbuttoned his shirt to move my hands down his chest, then his rippled abs. How the hell did he have time to keep a body this fit?

"I want to make you mine," Alex whispered against my lips. "Nikki, may I take you to the bedroom?"

A shudder ran through me, and I pulled away to search his eyes. "Yes, but..." I hesitated.

He smiled gently. "If it's too soon, just say so. It's okay."

I had to close my eyes in order to be able to spit it out. "I have a personal rule that I don't sleep with a guy unless we've been dating for six weeks."

Alex laughed, but thankfully he didn't seem irritated. He bounced me on his knee for a moment, breaking the tension. "Six weeks? Is this from one of those chick dating rulebooks or something?"

I giggled awkwardly. "No, I just want to be sure it's some kind of a real relationship before I go there."

He was still chuckling a bit. "Why six weeks? Why not seven?"

I shook my head, laughing with him. "Because the first guy I dated, I met him on New Year's Eve. And when I was thinking about what I felt was an appropriate amount of time to consider a relationship established, I figured how he reacted to Valentine's Day was reasonable. And that's six weeks and a day from New Year's."

He raised an eyebrow, studying my face. "So if he doesn't do the whole hearts and flowers commercial crap, he's not worthy?"

"No! Not at all." I wound my fingers in the back of his hair. "I don't care about that stuff. But some people have all of these weird perfect fantasies in their minds. I want a guy who can work with me to plan a holiday that suits both of us."

Alex suddenly looked devastated. "Nikki, I guess it's good that I'm pointing this out now. I can't ever promise that I'll be around for holidays. My schedule is sometimes unpredictable, sometimes outright insane. So sometimes I have to shift holidays around. Would you really care that much if we celebrated Valentine's Day on the twelfth? Or the seventeenth?"

I shook my head again. "Really, it's just an excuse to have a nice dinner together, right?"

He sighed heavily. "Thank goodness."

He kissed me again, gently, dreamily. The soft feeling of his lips gliding against mine made the blood dance through my veins.

"So," he said softly. "You don't want to have sex until we've been dating for six weeks. Are we counting that from our first amazing New Year's kiss?"

"Well..." I said, staring off into space thoughtfully for a moment before flashing him a grin. "Yeah, I think so."

"I know I've been away a lot, and technically it's only been three weeks. Tell me that means I'm at least allowed to take you to the bedroom, strip you naked, and lick you until you come on my tongue."

I gasped, my hand fluttering over my mouth.

He laughed, absolutely delighted by my reaction. "What? Has it been a while since a man has done that for you?"

I could feel my cheeks flaming.

"Oh my God – baby... Have you never had your pussy eaten properly?"

My eyes snapped closed again, and I wasn't sure why I was so embarrassed. "My sweet little innocent Nikki," he murmured against my ear. "We can wait as long as you like. Or, you can let your naughty new boyfriend take care of you right now. Would you like that?"

His hands were rubbing up and down my spine, causing me to dissolve into a little puddle. My chin tipped up and down before I even realized my body had made the decision independent of my brain.

"That's my girl," he said with a saucy grin.

Pulling me up, we went to the bedroom, and he immediately began undressing me, unwrapping me as if I were a work of art that he wanted to admire.

"You're so beautiful," he murmured, sliding off my shirt, my skirt, then standing back to stare at me in my light pink bra and panties.

"How did a guy like me get so lucky," he chuckled to himself, unhooking my bra and sliding it off gently.

His mouth latched around my nipple so quickly I gasped, clutching the back of his shoulders. His tongue lapped in circles around my sensitive skin, then I felt him sucking gently, sending chills straight through me. Moving to the other side, he did it again until I was quivering, my thighs pressing together.

I'd never been so flooded with arousal in my life, and my body was screaming for me to give myself to him completely.

Alex brought his head up to kiss me softly for a moment, then slipped off my panties. He sat me on the bed, spreading my legs wide as he dropped to his knees.

His lips nuzzled slowly up my inner thighs, switching from side to side until he was breathing against my most private skin. I was nervous, but also fascinated.

He spread my sensitive folds open with his thumbs, running his fingertips all along my skin while I tried not to squirm.

"Nikki, I'm certainly not an expert, but I am positive that this is the prettiest, sweetest little pussy on earth."

I tried to think of a clever response, but he flattened his tongue against my open flesh, licking upward steadily until he swept across my clit. My squealing moans surprised me, as my fingers clutched the back of his hair.

"Relax, baby," he murmured. "Just let it all go."

It was so strangely intimate, and I was almost surprised I was able to let Alex touch me like this. I was nervous, but he seemed to care for me so much. I almost giggled when I realized that his only goal was to make me happy.

Alex made a low growl deep in his throat as he stared up at me, licking up my juices. "So wet for me," he murmured, then he swirled his tongue all around my throbbing clit. I gasped, trying to keep my hips still.

He brought one of his large hands down on my hip bone, pinning me to keep me steady. With his other hand, he traced along my outer pussy lips, then ran his tongue all along every fold as I moaned and squirmed under him.

"You're so sexy, Nikki," he murmured, dipping the tip of his thick middle finger into the opening of my pussy lips. "Is this what you want, baby?"

His finger sunk inside me just an inch, and I moaned loudly, gripping his hair as I shivered. The intensity of the feelings flowing through me was far too much to process. He flashed me a breathtaking grin, his deep blue eyes blazing as he wandered his finger inside me. Locking his tongue onto my swollen clit, he began lapping steadily.

It felt like liquid heat was flowing through every part of my body, as my quivering became shaking. My fingers clutched his head too tightly as I held him against me, rubbing my entire pussy against his mouth and hand as I completely lost control.

"Alex... Oh my God... yes!" I wailed as I came shamelessly against his tongue. My body lurched, tensing and twitching under him.

When I collapsed back onto the bed, he pulled his finger out of me slowly, sliding into his mouth as he sucked it clean. Then he was on top of me, fully clothed even though I was naked, his hot mouth against mine as he kissed me endlessly.

Before I realized what was going on, I was on top of him, squirming and grinding, my body positively begging for his.

"Damn, you are a sexy thing," he growled, clutching the back of my hair to hold me still so he could kiss me more deeply.

Then he grabbed my hips where I was helplessly rocking against the intimidating bulge in his jeans. "Not tonight, baby," he smiled, reaching out to stroke my hair. "I'm not going to let you break your own rules just because you got all riled up."

I was grateful that his self-control was obviously a bit more advanced than mine. "I'm sorry," I whispered, reaching a hand to his chest. Then I let it slide lower, feeling his abs along the way.

He grabbed my wrist as I reached his pants. "Not tonight," he said. "Soon. But right now, after hearing your hot little noises, I honestly don't know whether I could control myself with you here naked." He shot me a playful wink, then sat up, pulling me into his arms for a kiss that knocked all of the air from my body.

"I'm going to go before I talk you into letting me stay over, because there's no way I can keep my hands off you," he said gently.

He wrapped me in a blanket so that I could walk him to the door. "I think I have jobs in town for a couple of days, but can't remember at the moment. I'll text you tomorrow, okay?"

"Sure."

Alex gently kissed me again. "Sweet dreams, gorgeous."

I locked the door behind him then floated back to bed, still not quite sure I believed what had just happened. I felt like my entire life had been turned upside down. Every normal routine and schedule had been kicked to the curb to make way for this incredible man.

It was weird. It felt perfectly right, but there was some paranoid voice in the back of my brain that questioned whether I should really trust everything so much, since we hadn't really spent a lot of time together. Yet when we were together, everything felt so right. Maybe I just had to believe.

10

*** ALEX ***

As much as I was positively dying to make love with her, part of me found it unbelievably precious that Nikki wanted to wait. It confirmed my feeling that she was a good girl. A sweet girl. Someone who wanted a real relationship, and was in it for the long haul, not just a fling.

A girl like her might take the time to understand my weird schedules and bizarre life. She won't run away the first second things get difficult.

But I also wondered how much experience she had with men. If I happened to be the first guy she dated past the six week mark, that was a lot of pressure. I hoped that I could live up to whatever expectations she might have.

I knew that sex was very different between men and women, and that women attached a much greater emotional significance to the act. For the first time in my life, that was genuinely what I wanted as well. I didn't want to just throw her down and have fun.

I needed to bond with her. Watch her eyes as she felt

new things. I wanted to smile with her as she experienced all sorts of pleasure.

Perhaps it would destroy my reputation as a bit of a tough guy, someone who never got rattled no matter what hit him. But I was already in love with Nikki. She already had my heart.

11

* NIKKI *

My mind and body were reeling from Alex's intensity. He seemed so absolutely certain that we were already a real couple. It was wild and overwhelming.

He had jobs in the city for the next few days, but during weird hours. We sent random texts here and there, mostly about our work, and the importance of coffee to our productivity.

For the next few days, I went back to my regular life of planning and scheduling. As expected, work picked up, and our whole office ended up working late on Tuesday and Wednesday.

It was wonderful how the teams all came together bouncing around and helping each other as much as possible. I even found my boss, Matt, in the boardroom with pages spread everywhere, assisting with the proofreading.

We ordered in Chinese food on Tuesday, pizza on Wednesday, and Thursday around four pm I realized that we still had at least four hours of work to do. I ignored my phone beeping as I went around to take everyone's order from our favorite Indian restaurant.

Once the food was on its way, and I had made a quick list of essential tasks that absolutely had to be finished before we left this evening, I checked my phone.

Hey gorgeous, I have tonight off! May I take you out to dinner? I haven't taken my beautiful girl out on a real date yet, and I don't want to be a bad boyfriend.

I felt absolutely horrible. I actually thought about leaving for half a second, but there was no way I could abandon the team. I replied immediately.

I'm so sorry, but this is our super busy week. I'm going to be stuck at the office until at least eight or nine.

That sucks, baby. But I totally understand. I'm leaving for Seattle at five in the morning. Back in a week. I'll call you when I can. Hope that your huge workload goes smoothly for you.

Alex was obviously a dedicated worker, and I knew that he would completely understand that I couldn't take off at a moment's notice. So I didn't know why I felt guilty. Perhaps it was actually just disappointment that I wouldn't get to see him for so long.

I missed him already. I missed the way I felt when I was with him. As much as I truly enjoyed chatting with him in our endless texts, it wasn't nearly the same as having him hold me.

Patience is not a virtue that I particularly wanted to work on this year. On the other hand, I had sworn off men, and was determined to break my New Year's to Valentine's curse.

A cold, prickly feeling settled through my stomach, as I tried to catch up on organizing the rest of the office tasks. If we rarely saw each other, would Alex and I even make it to Valentine's Day? I knew he was interested in me, but was he going to be all right with this strange, slow pace?

Thinking about it would just send me spiraling into a tornado of anxiety, so I tried to put it out of my mind and just to get through the day.

The next morning I woke up to a text with a photo of Alex holding up my duck magnet in front of the Pearson Airport sign. About six hours later, I got another photo of them in front of a sign that said, "Welcome to Seattle."

I replied with a photo taken from the edge of my desk, looking up at the looming tower of folders filled with projects.

He replied a few hours later with a selfie taken while holding up a Starbucks coffee cup with the duck sitting on top. Then I looked over his shoulder to see Starbucks corporate headquarters.

I burst out laughing so loudly that my coworkers actually turned around to stare at me as if I'd lost my mind.

The next few days were a blur of long hours, even bringing my work laptop home to put in a few hours Saturday morning. It was as if I was back to my regular life, but now I had this secret, adorable, possibly imaginary boyfriend to text and call.

I was now always looking for opportunities to take funny little photos of my life to send him. At the end of every day, I sent him a report of the good things that happened.

Strangely, by documenting my life like this every day, it was making me realize how unbelievably grateful I was for everything I had. I didn't quite know how to thank Alex for that, but it was cool to notice that he was truly a positive influence on my world.

12

*** ALEX ***

The disappointment I felt when I couldn't take Nikki out for dinner was much more soul-crushing than I had anticipated. But of all people, I certainly understood that work came first.

I wanted to feel like we were growing closer, but this week-long trip was the worst timing ever. It was a relief that she texted and sent a lot of photos. I did feel connected to her. It just wasn't enough. My feelings for her were making me greedy, and I wanted so much more.

All I could do was hang on until next week, and somehow find a way to spend as much quality time with her as possible.

Even though I was running around at work fixing broken equipment, hauling speakers, running cables, and updating tragically out of date software on my client's systems, I was also sending as many photos as possible with Nikki's duck.

Strangely, he was becoming my little buddy. We had breakfast together, he sat on my pillow when I was getting ready for bed, and I pulled him out at every photo opportunity. I sort of felt like he was Nikki's pet, and I was taking care of him.

When I told her this, she sent a text that was a string of hearts. Luckily, this reminded me that Valentine's Day was coming, and I was going to have to prove myself worthy. I couldn't ever let her be disappointed on that holiday again.

13
___

* NIKKI *

Through our strange text-based conversations, and the process of getting to know Alex, I was impressed that he never talked down to me. He would explain some of the more technical aspects of what he did, and he didn't gloss over the details. If I was confused, I asked more questions. But he never treated me like a girl who wouldn't understand.

I found that admirable. Even though I wasn't quite as fascinated with acoustics, and the timing when sound traveled through a huge auditorium, it was really interesting. Maybe it was healthy that we were learning about each other intellectually more than physically.

But I couldn't wait to see him. I knew he was coming back to Toronto soon, but he hadn't told me the exact date or time of his flight.

It seemed that our busy spell was pretty much over at the very end of January. I went home Friday night looking forward to an evening spent curled up on the couch watching movies.

Instead, I saw Alex and his suitcase on the steps of my apartment building.

In seconds I was lost in his kiss, in his arms. He held me so tightly, while his lips glided seductively against mine. For a second I wasn't even sure I could handle the amount of heat between us.

When he finally pulled away, he was laughing. "Hi. How are you?"

I laughed with him as we went inside, dropping our things and kicking off our shoes. But instead of heading for the couch, Alex took my hand and led me straight to the bedroom.

"I've missed you so much, baby," he murmured into my neck as he kissed down my throat. I stepped back to pull my sweater over my head, chuckling at my hair instantly turning into a disaster of static.

"I missed you too," I said, unbuttoning his shirt.

Normally I would feel completely shy undressing with a man, but at the moment all I felt was pure desire.

Before I even realized what was happening, I had been stripped to my panties, and he was wearing only a pair of black briefs. He laid down, pulling me on top of him, kissing me with a fiery passion that caused every inch of me to tingle.

"Damn, you're sexy," he growled, grabbing my ass and grinding against me while I squirmed against him.

My body was reacting so hard, so fast, that I felt my nipples tighten, my pussy almost dripping with need. Alex held me against him as if he were drawing energy from everywhere we were touching.

"I'm sorry I've been gone so much, Nikki. It'll be better in a couple of weeks. My work will never be normal, but I'll be able to see you more regularly."

"Good," I murmured, my lips traveling down his neck to kiss across the broad expanse of his huge chest.

I realized with surprise that I needed to please him. To taste him. To make him lose control. Continuing down his chest, he reached under me to massage my breasts, twirling his thumbs around my nipples as I moaned softly from his touch.

Then I moved lower, kissing down his stomach until my hand pressed against the very obvious outline in his shorts.

Alex chuckled. "You can just ignore that, if you like. I am mainly concerned with snuggling and kissing you enough."

Looking up, I flashed him a wink. "I'm curious," I said, then I pulled the fabric around his hips and down his legs, leaving him naked.

Tentatively wrapping my hands around his thick shaft, I stroked gently. I'd never touched a guy without clothing between us before, and was astounded by how his skin was strangely soft, but the surface underneath was extremely firm. It was also a bit larger than I expected, but he was a pretty big guy. It felt like it was coming alive under my touch, as I moved my fingers up and down carefully.

Alex reached out to stroke my hair, giving me an encouraging grin. "That feels amazing."

He settled into the bed, his thighs falling open as he relaxed completely. I experimented, watching his eyes as I gripped tighter, then moved faster or slower.

"I think I like it when you check out my special toy," he winked.

He was so ridiculously handsome, and completely comfortable in his own body, that the urge to please him bubbled up inside me even stronger.

Looking down, I saw a clear drop of pre-cum bead at the

round head of his cock. Without even thinking, I bent forward to lick it.

A shudder ran through him, making me grin. Leaning in, I wrapped my lips around the head, letting my tongue wander around his skin as I angled his length toward me. Slowly slipping my lips down his shaft, his soft moan absolutely thrilled me. Knowing that I was arousing him this much was wild.

Moving my hands along the base, and my lips up and down the top, I covered every inch of his cock with my attention.

"Wow," he whispered. His eyes were riveted on me, watching every tiny motion I made.

I could feel his excitement building, and his cock seemed to thicken even more.

"Nikki," he said gently, "You don't have to swallow if you don't want to."

I was grateful for the warning, but I wanted to see his reaction. I gripped tighter, pressing my lips more firmly as I worked his entire shaft faster.

Alex made a low moaning noise, stroking the back of my hair gently as I moved even faster. "Oh fuck... Nikki..." he choked, then my mouth was flooded with salty heat. Swallowing quickly, I continued sucking and licking until he stopped quivering, and collapsed back onto the bed.

I crawled up to lay beside him, and he instantly grabbed me, kissing me hard and deep.

"That was amazing, baby," he murmured. "I haven't felt anything that good in a very long time."

I grinned against his kiss, loving the feeling of his arms so tight around me. I just wanted to dissolve into his chest and stay that way forever. Then I was flipped onto my back, squealing as his lips wrapped around my nipple, sucking gently. I gasped, my hands wandering across the back of his shoulders as I clutched him against me.

He moved to the other side, sucking and licking while his hand slipped lower until he was cupping the center of my panties.

Alex looked up at me, his eyes burning. "I love that you're so wet for me, Nikki." His finger traced along the soaking fabric as I shivered from his gentle touch. "Do you want me to pull these off and lick your sweet little pussy?"

I could feel myself blushing, but nodded.

Suddenly my head was tipped back as he kissed along my throat. "You're so shy, gorgeous. Let me hear you say it." He looked at me expectantly, but I honestly didn't think I could speak.

He kissed along the side of my jaw, skipped over my lips, then kissed along my cheekbone on the other side. "Just say it, baby. Do you want your naughty boyfriend to lick your sexy pussy until you squeal?"

Grabbing the back of his head, I pulled his lips to mine, writhing under him as I kissed him desperately.

"Sassy little thing," he grinned. "Just say it, Nikki. Tell me what you want."

His fingertips slid back and forth through my soaking pussy lips, pressing the silky fabric against me. "Do you want me to take these off?" he asked.

"Yes, please," I whispered.

"Then what do you want?" he smirked, his eyebrow raised. He turned so that his ear was directly against my lips.

He was just teasing, trying to push me out of my comfort zone. He might not even have known how intoxicatingly sexy he was being by forcing me to say something I would never have imagined saying in a million years.

"Alex," I barely breathed, "Would you please lick my pussy?"

Turning his head, he kissed me so hard I was almost breathless. "I'm proud of you, sweetheart."

His mouth returned to my breast, sucking as much of my flesh into his mouth as he could while flicking my other nipple with his thumb. Sparks of both pleasure and anticipation danced up my spine, then he began kissing down my ribs, and across my stomach. How did he make me feel so proud of myself for such little things?

Hooking his thumbs into the sides of my panties, he slowly pulled them off, and I was almost embarrassed at how soaked they were. I was twitching as he spread my thighs.

Then his tongue swept vertically against my pussy lips and clit, and all thoughts in my mind vanished. My fingers wandered through his thick hair, not pulling, just caressing.

I loved how he took his time exploring my skin, warming me straight through. I loved the way he was so gentle, so careful as he lapped at my clit as if it were candy. I adored how he carefully slid two thick fingers inside me, filling me. The pressure was incredible, and my hips began to squirm with need.

I felt so close to him, giving him complete control of my body. It felt right. As if I were meant to be this relaxed all the time, while invisible flames swirled through my core.

There was something powerful about the way his eyes locked on mine as he pressed his tongue against my nerves, licking steadily. He must have been able to feel my body tightening, locking up, as the intoxicating wave washed through me. "Alex... Yes!" I screamed, shaking as everything overloaded in a blaze of pure pleasure.

Once I'd caught my breath, he laid beside me, holding

me close. "Hey," he whispered, "Can I stay the night? No sex, I promise. I just want to hold you. Be near you."

"Mmm, yes," I murmured. I was already falling asleep, my head resting perfectly into a little nook on his chest at the front of his shoulder.

14

———————

* ALEX *

Spending so many hours with Nikki's soft, curvy body in my arms was pure heaven. Glancing down at her precious doll face, I was struck by a flash of absolute gratitude. I was thankful that I'd seen her that night. That I'd been so drawn to her that I ignored all rules of polite social convention and just kissed her. And that I'd found her again.

She was so sweet, so understanding. But her patience with me was completely remarkable. I knew I was a difficult person to deal with. I fell asleep in the middle of text conversations, and it was hard to schedule anything with me. Yet Nikki didn't take this personally. I'm sure she was disappointed now and then, but she was mature and sensible enough to understand that it wasn't about her.

As she slowly woke up, I stroked her back gently. It was wonderful that she stayed naked with me all night. I thought that she might get shy and grab a nightgown. There was something about bonding with skin against skin that made me feel even more connected to her.

I knew from the first second I saw her that she was my

girl. But waking up with her in my arms, feeling so grounded, so relaxed with her, confirmed my gut reaction.

"Mmm, hi," she whispered.

Glancing over her shoulder at the clock, I began to laugh.

"What?" she giggled softly.

Nuzzling her neck, I sighed. "I can't think of the last time I didn't set an alarm. I'm glad your sweet sexiness woke me up. I have to leave in twenty minutes."

"No," she pouted dramatically, placing her hand in the center of my chest. "I want my pillow man to stay."

"You're so sexy when you're sleepy," I said, then I pulled her up a bit so that I could kiss her.

Sliding one hand down to cup her sexy round ass, my other hand trailed gently around her breasts until I sensed that tiny change in her breathing. Gliding my hand lower, I gravitated straight to her softness, sliding one finger into her inner lips, toying with her until she moaned in my arms.

Placing two fingertips directly on her clit, I moved in slow, gentle circles. Her eyes flew wide, then her long, low sigh tugged at my heart.

Our kiss grew deeper as she began to twitch. Watching Nikki grow flushed, squirming against me, was the hottest thing I'd ever seen. She was so fair that her cheeks easily became pink, her breathing becoming uneven.

"You're so pretty when you come for me," I murmured against her lips.

She couldn't hold her eyes open, shaking, alternating between gasping and kissing me almost roughly. "Oh," she nearly whined, "Oh... Alex... Ah!"

Feeling her explode against my hand, my chest, my lips, was so erotic I could nearly have come just from the sight of her.

"I love it when you let go for me, baby," I whispered, kissing her cheeks, her nose. Then I leaned back to watch her eyes. "Tomorrow morning when I'm not here, I want you to do that for yourself, and think of me."

Nikki giggled, turning her head into my shoulder shyly.

"Okay," I laughed, "Just think about it."

I kissed her again, then reluctantly rolled away, tucking her in completely as I found my clothes. "Will the front door lock after I close it?"

"Yeah."

I leaned in to give her one last kiss. "I have to upgrade someone's sound system this afternoon, then teach them how to use it at a show tonight. Then I'm flying out in the morning. I'll text you soon."

"Okay. I'll miss you."

"I'll miss you more than you could ever believe," I said gently. Then I left quickly before I was tempted to crawl back into bed with her.

15

---

* NIKKI *

The next few weeks were a blur of texts, phone calls, and a ton of work. There weren't many more late nights, but everyone was a bit on edge from the amount of work flowing through. Matt even started placing the stickers from his apples and bananas in patterns on the cabinets of the coffee room, which he only did when he was stressed out.

Finally everything was under control, and I was hit with a different kind of stress. It was February eleventh, and I hadn't seen Alex in a while. He'd been to Miami to work audio for a conference where people were pitching new television shows to networks. He went to Brooklyn to work with the audio-video team for a huge arts event. Then he was off to Montreal to supervise the setup of a new sound system for a small theatre.

Through it all, he sent me photos of him and my duck having grand adventures. It was adorable to me that he seemed to find little elements of each city that made him feel comfortable. He'd have a favorite coffee shop near the venue, and a neat restaurant he went to every time he was there.

It seemed like he was a homebody at heart, he just had to go about it in a very different way. But when he was at his real home, he was there just long enough to wash his clothes, repack his gear bag for the next job, sleep for a few hours, then take off again.

He swore that past February sixteenth or so, he only had one away gig per month until at least June.

Getting to know each other remotely was a bit strange, but it was also easier for me to really open up. I was able to think about things before I said them, and I was less likely to blush from embarrassment and shyness when he asked me personal questions. Like when he confirmed that I was on the pill, but I was, indeed a virgin.

Sometimes we'd get into a quick text discussion, and I'd find myself confessing things I'd never admit to anyone else, like my liking the fact that he was ten years older than me, and that I was surprised that I liked feeling so tiny and safe in his arms.

We finally arranged a date for February twelfth, but Alex warned me that he was leaving for Winnipeg early on the morning of February fourteenth.

I was more relieved than I had expected. With no Valentine pressure, we could just have a nice dinner and catch up in person.

When I walked into Alex's apartment for the first time, I was stunned to see pink fairy lights, red roses on the table, and him wearing a bright red tie with his black shirt.

Before I even got a chance to look around properly, he was already kissing me. "Happy early Valentine's Day, Nikki," he murmured, holding me close. I breathed him in, feeling that instant, perfect connection.

Then he sat me on the couch and poured us some champagne in front of a bowl of heart shaped dark chocolates and strawberries. It was wonderful and cheesy, and suddenly I felt really wrong about it.

"All of this hearts and flowers stuff isn't you, is it?" I could feel my bottom lip trembling, and was frustrated that I felt so rattled. "Alex, I can't ask you to change who you are. It's not right."

"It's okay," he said gently, slipping an arm around me. "I thought this was fun. To be honest, I've never had a chance to do something like this."

"But–"

"It's just a little bit of bending. Not changing, very slightly tweaking," he said quickly. "I can tell that you are the sort of person that works well with routines and systems. And yet here you are, ready to deal with my crazy life. You've never once complained. You've always made the best of everything. I really appreciate that. So I am more than happy to tweak a few things to make you happy."

His sweet smile made me completely melt. "I'm sorry I've been away so much."

"That wasn't your fault, I understand," I said, snuggling into his shoulder

"I know things have been up and down and weird between us, Nikki, but I want to really be your guy. Most of my longer trips are over until next season, and I can't guarantee that I can schedule anything in advance, but I want you to know that you're my priority as much as possible."

"I understand you can't turn down a gig," I said. "And if you have to cancel something last minute, I'll be disappointed, but I can shake that off in a minute, I swear."

He held my face in his hands. "I love how mellow you are. You're adaptable. You can learn to go with the flow.

You're the girl I need to bring me balance." He kissed me lightly, then grinned. "Like how you just rolled with it for that astounding New Year's kiss."

I couldn't help giggling. "That was so unlike me. I honestly cannot believe I kissed a stranger."

Alex nuzzled the side of my cheek. "I was never a stranger. I'm the love of your life, you just hadn't met me yet." He kissed the tip of my nose, grinning. "So, can we be all hearts and flowers and cheesy now? Will you be my damn Valentine and make everything official?"

"Yes," I whispered, kissing him lightly.

He pulled out a box, opening it to reveal a lovely gold necklace with a charm of two hearts entwined. "I looked for a duck, but they didn't have one," he chuckled.

He fastened the chain around my neck, then looked at me quite seriously. "I want you to wear something of mine as much as possible. I'm fully aware that it sounds possessive. I'm going to work on that, but for the moment, let me claim you. Okay?"

I nodded. There was no way for me to tell him that I adored the way he was so possessive with me. It felt so good compared to guys who didn't care at all. He was just intense. But he did grow, and he did listen. And he was committed to keeping a close connection with us, even when he wasn't here in person.

"Yes," I whispered, nodding.

His hand slid into the back of my hair, pulling my lips to his for a kiss so scorching that I nearly lost my breath.

"I'd really like it if you'd spend the night," he whispered. "I'll behave myself, I promise."

"No."

His face fell. "Oh. Do you have to work early or something?"

"No, um... I mean, I want to stay. I don't want you to behave yourself."

He looked at me carefully. "It hasn't been six weeks."

Throwing my arms around him, I kissed him in a way that screamed the things I couldn't say. I felt the shift in him as he understood me. My lips parted gently and he took the hint, his tongue softly meeting mine as his hands slid up my shirt to stroke my back.

Then he pulled away. "Did you want dinner? Or some champagne?"

Looking into his deep eyes, I realized what I was truly hungry for. I wanted to make us even more official. There was already a bond between us deeper than anyone I'd ever known. I wanted to take the extra step.

Shocking myself with my complete lack of shyness for once in my life, I took his hand. "Dinner later. Show me your bedroom?"

His grin nearly knocked me sideways. He led me to a tiny room with a huge bed, and I laughed at the blackout curtains. "For sleeping during the middle of the day?" He chuckled and nodded. Then his mouth began sucking gently along the side of my neck as he pulled my clothing off.

I was naked and on my back before I knew it, his hungry stare locked on my body as he pulled his clothes off. He laid down with me, and our kissing and cuddling had a new level of heat behind it.

I've always been nervous whenever a man touched me, but not now. I realized with absolute certainty that he wasn't just a man anymore. He was the one. He was mine, and I was his. There were no more questions that needed to be answered.

Alex's hands caressed every inch of my skin, making

everything tingle as my pulse began to race. My body was reacting in a way he must have been able to feel.

I almost felt that I should be embarrassed at how wet I was, as he slipped his hand between my thighs, teasing gently as he circled my entrance.

I could see a shudder run through him. "I love that your body is so ready for me, Nikki." Then he examined my eyes carefully. "Are you sure you really want this now? We can wait if you want."

I shook my head. "Alex, I want you. Completely."

That adorable handsome grin made me giggle, then gasp as he slid a finger inside me. Then a second.

Feeling him slowly thrusting in and out, my hips begin to squirm. But then he brought his thumb to my clit, and I realized I was far too close to the edge already. Gripping the back of his neck, I pulled him to me, kissing him hard.

Moaning shamelessly into his mouth, I felt the tension gathering deep within me, about to lose control completely. My legs fell open as he moved his hand faster, then suddenly I was falling, squealing against his lips as my climax rumbled through my entire body, making me shake.

Alex grinned in delight, his eyes wide. Then his gaze became dreamy, softer. He laid over me, and I could feel his arousal pressed tightly against my hip bone.

"Nikki, I've never wanted to be someone's first before. I thought I'd be too nervous. But I love you so much, and I just want to feel everything with you."

I felt my breath catch as I looked up at him, completely overwhelmed. "I love you, Alex. I want to feel you, too."

Feeling him rubbing the thick head of his shaft between my open, swollen pussy lips sent deep shivers through me. It was hard to keep my hips still as he eased inside me a little, kissing me gently.

"Mmm, more," I murmured.

He pressed in further, as I heard his low groan. "Baby, you're so soft, but so tight."

He eased in slowly, and I was so wet that it didn't really hurt, it was just a strange deep pressure. Alex was incredibly gentle, and must have had amazing self-control.

He cupped my cheek with one hand, dotting kisses all across my forehead and cheeks as he began rocking slowly back and forth, filling me completely. I truly felt like I was giving myself to him, the closeness between us so much greater than our bodies.

He grabbed my hip with one hand, his gentle rhythm increasing slightly as my body opened for his. His long, deep strokes were creating sensations inside me that I'd never dreamed of before, as he grazed my clit with every movement.

My hips begin to rock, moving up against him to pull him even deeper. I saw his eyes flash with delight as I moved with him. Wrapping my legs around his hips, a shuddering moan escaped me as I quivered.

"You feel so perfect, gorgeous," he whispered, moving just a little faster.

Looking up into his expressive eyes, I could feel that this meant as much to him as it did to me.

"I love you," I choked, my body beginning to almost burn from pleasure.

"I love you, Nikki," he said gently, then he kissed me deeply, his tongue sliding into my mouth to match the movements of our bodies together.

My hips were lifting off the bed, pulling him deeper as we writhed together. Our moans filled the room, as my hands slid down his back to grip his ass tightly.

"You feel so perfect around me," he whispered, and

somehow knowing that I was pleasing him made me lose all control. My entire body lurched as I started to climax, wiggling and squealing under him as he thrust faster.

"Oh, Nikki... Yes..." he moaned, then I felt him jerk inside me, his throbbing cock filling me with his heat as he came.

We trembled together until he finally leaned up on his elbows to take his weight off me.

He looked down and at me in absolute wonder. "Nikki, I can't believe how sexy you are. And that you're all mine. Forever."

I couldn't control my giggling, and he sat up, pulling me against him as we snuggled.

I wanted to tell him how utterly perfect that had been, but I couldn't find words. So I simply stared at him for a moment, before kissing him gently.

"My unbelievably sweet, smart, adorable girl," he chuckled, rocking me against him. "I promise to feed you in a couple of minutes, but right now, I just need to hold you."

"We have all the time in the world," I murmured. "Even when our schedules get messed up, we'll just keep on trying again."

"I love that you understand, baby," he said softly, kissing the top of my head. "I'm so lucky that I found you."

"And that I found you again," I laughed.

EPILOGUE
* NIKKI *

One Year and Three Days Later

I woke up in a strange place, and had to look around for a moment before I realized where and when it was. Fancy hotel room. Alex's arm curled around me. February fifteenth, the morning after our wedding.

He had jokingly said it was the first holiday he actually booked off. For the past year, every holiday and occasion had been moved around his schedule, but that was okay. It was sort of like we were in our own alternate reality, where Thanksgiving was on Tuesday, and birthdays were simply the nearest convenient weekend.

I actually enjoyed having our Christmas dinner on December twenty-third, and went with him to his in-town job on the twenty-fifth as his 'assistant'. It was a super easy day, and I learned a lot about what he actually did while making myself useful fetching coffee for the crew, and carefully curating a light lounge music playlist for the cocktail hour before the giant dinner, when they switched to a live jazz trio.

Honestly, although it was completely non-traditional to me, being with Alex made it fun and festive.

When he had proposed a week later on New Year's Day, telling me that he was booking Valentine's Day off for our wedding, I was stunned. But it was perfect.

It didn't matter that it seemed like a short engagement, and getting married so soon seemed like a rush. Our timing and schedules had always been completely off-kilter. It didn't matter. We always ended up together, and deliriously happy. It was also a great excuse to keep things small and intimate, so that we actually had a wonderful time.

"Good morning, gorgeous. What are you smiling about?" Alex asked, propping himself up on an elbow as he brushed my hair out of my eyes.

"You know," I drawled sleepily. "Just thankful that I'll never have to stress out about Valentine's Day again."

Alex's thick arms wrapped around me, rocking me gently. "Why did you stress, baby?"

"I didn't, really. It was just a stupid yearly reminder that I hadn't found someone yet."

He chuckled. "And now you're stuck with me forever."

"Apparently, yes."

Reaching under the blankets, he grabbed my ass, giving me the tiniest smack. "Come on, wife, where's my breakfast?"

The glare I fired at him made him jump back with his hands raised. "Kidding, of course! What can I order for my darling princess?"

Sitting up, I fluffed my hair. "Pancakes, a cheese omelet, coffee, and mimosas."

Alex's adorable grin lit up both his face and his body language as he perked up and reached for the room service menu. "Good idea. It's only really a vacation if you drink booze before noon."

"Precisely."

"Plus, I'll get to toast my gorgeous new bride."

"Oh yeah – whole wheat toast."

He looked at me cautiously. "Nikki, you've been eating a lot more over the past few weeks. Is there any chance…"

I laughed so loudly I cut him off. "I'm not pregnant! I just stress-eat when I'm overwhelmed."

It surprised me that his face fell. "Oh."

Still giggling, I gave him a kiss. "Let's hang out and be married for a couple of years before kids, okay?"

He stuck his bottom lip out in a silly pout. "But I want to see your curves get even curvier. I want to hear you sing little songs to our baby, and watch you try to put them on a schedule so I can laugh when it never works."

I adored the way he made me giggle. "Okay, but when we're ready, we'll carefully plan so that you can take a few months of just in-town jobs when the baby comes. I'm going to need you close by."

"I promise."

My mouth fell open. "That's the first time you've ever promised anything about your schedule."

He grinned. "And the wedding. I wasn't going to miss that."

"Okay, that too."

His thumb traced my bottom lip as those dark blue eyes held my gaze. "I love you so much, crazy Valentine wife."

"I love you, wacky New Year's kiss husband."

The menu fell from his hand as he pulled me against him, our kiss, and his hands on my skin, suddenly much more important than breakfast.

SNEAK PREVIEW

Excerpt from *The Lumberjack's Quirky Girl*

Facing the woods directly beside the parking lot, I admire the greenery, still stretching out my shoulders. Last night I was hunched over my art table, painting for hours. The night before that I was retouching photos, and the night before I was studying photography tips until two in the morning. Yeah, I know. Being a multi-disciplinary artist with poor impulse control squashes any hope of a consistent sleep schedule, but I wouldn't have it any other way.

My head swivels when I hear a metallic thump. A huge man is standing on the back bumper of a pickup, leaning over to search for something. Worn denim stretches perfectly over his sculpted ass.

My mouth falls open in shock as I stare. His sturdy legs bend and flex as he finds whatever he was looking for and lightly jumps down to the ground. He turns and smiles when he sees me, and now—

Oh my.

I don't know where to look. Perfect teeth. Gorgeous, sultry eyes. Tall, huge frame, at least six foot four.

He chuckles. "Were you staring at my axe?"

Did he say...

Blinking hard, I realize he's referring to the massive wood-handled axe leaning on the back of the truck, not his spectacular behind.

My head shakes as I try to think of something appropriate to say. "Nice axe."

Oh my... I did *not* just say that. He laughs out loud. Hopefully my pink cheeks are partially hidden as I dip my head.

Slipping the axe into its holster, he puts it away, clanking against the metal bed of his mud-spattered pickup. He approaches, brushing his hands off against his well-muscled thighs straining against his jeans. "I know, that thing looks a bit sinister."

If he is still subtly referring to his body, he's right. His thick arms look like they could pick me up and hurl me out to the highway like he was tossing a caber. And his snug t-shirt is getting a workout just stretching across that broad chest.

This man is the most stunning, seductive creature I've ever laid eyes on, and if I don't start speaking like a normal person soon, he'll figure out that I'm a weirdo. "I'm just hoping that you aren't about to cut any trees down right here." I wave to the wooded area beside us.

His incredible body plops itself casually into the patio chair beside me. "Nope. Got my own forest." He holds out his hand. "Braden Oakley."

His warm, firm palm presses against mine as I try not to hold it longer than the regulation three seconds. I fail, clasping his hand for at least a five count. "Elise Laurent." As I let my hand drop, his name clicks. "The huge forest Oakleys?"

His rich chuckle is causing a flutter in the center of my chest. "Yes on both counts. My family owns the land the forest is on, and my three brothers and I are all pretty big."

"I thought you all moved away?"

Sweet fancy fairies... That smile. My body leans closer without my brain telling it to.

It's odd that he's looking so deeply into my eyes, as if he's trying to analyze me. Although, to be fair, there aren't that many women in Oakton with pink streaked hair and sporting neon green dangling dragonfly earrings.

"We're coming back."

I can't tell if he's happy about that or not. "Not entirely your choice, is it?"

His hand reaches to his throat in an automatic gesture, then awkwardly pulls away.

I burst out laughing. "You can't straighten a tie that isn't there. Are you used to wearing a suit all day?"

His perfect lips stretch into a brilliant grin. "Busted. Yeah, my brothers and I are all moving back to tend the property ourselves."

"So you've gone from businessman to...lumberjack?" I'm suddenly picturing him in a suit, and my knees press together. Did he just walk around offices looking gorgeous like that all day long?

"Pretty much." Braden's impressive shoulders come closer as he leans in. His hazel eyes lock on mine, making my breath unsteady. "Tell me something about yourself, Elise. Something that nobody else knows."

For a split second, my mind achieves a level of total

emptiness that no meditation class has ever managed to. "Today's word of the day in my calendar was 'dastardly' and I've been trying to use it in a sentence." *Yikes.* There goes any chance of him thinking I was cool.

Yet Braden grins. "Well, then. How would you describe a man who is ruining what is clearly your break time?"

I grin back. "Dastardly?"

"What about a man who asks a girl out after only having known her for..." He checks his big tactical gadgety watch. "Three minutes?"

I wait for the punchline, but there isn't one. "Um, I'm gonna go with dastardly?"

He reaches out to lift my hand, kissing the back of it so sweetly that I nearly lose the ability to breathe. "What time are you done work?"

My evening plans of examining every setting on my new camera lens instantly disappear. "Six."

"Can I pick you up then?"

My mind has officially checked out, leaving me on auto-pilot. "Sure."

"Have a great day, Elise. I'll see you later."

"Yeah. Okay." Not my most eloquent comeback, but at least it's in English.

Floating inside, I head straight to the bathroom to confirm that indeed I'm flushed. At least my hair isn't doing anything particularly stupid. *Wow.* I have a date with a man I just met. More specifically, one of the mysterious Oakley men. The most gorgeous man I've ever set eyes on.

A man who instantly makes me think lusty, carnal thoughts that are definitely dastardly.

Stay tuned for
The Lumberjack's Quirky Girl
The Lumberjack's Curvy Girl
The Lumberjack's Shy Girl
The Lumberjack's Nerdy Girl
~ January through March 2023 ~

ALSO BY HALEY TRAVIS

Her New Bodyguard: Jackson

It was supposed to be a simple personal security job. But Ashley was so sexy and innocent that my need to care for her was far more than professional. She was sunshine and warmth and everything I truly desired. She felt like... home.

Mackton Mechanics

Rev your engines and get ready to fall for these hot mechanics! These huge, rough men are comfortable working with steel. What will happen when they're tinkering with a sweet girl's heart instead of a motor?

Never Date The Boss

Ashley was talked into one little "business date" with her boss, and everything changed in a heartbeat. Or rather, a flutter of them.

Daddy's Billionaire Boss

When Emily discovers her Dad's boss is the improbable man her aunt predicted she'd fall for, can she fit into his world?

Mr. Right... As Rain

A gorgeous man saved me on the way to an interview. Maybe it was the good luck kiss from a stranger, but isn't falling in love so fast just a fantasy?

Fake Summer Boyfriend

I'm terrified of giant men. But when Leif volunteered to scare off my stalker by pretending to be my boyfriend, I knew the gorgeous hulking security tech was the perfect man for the job.

Lights, Camera, Lies

When Alice pretends to be Taylor's wife to win a TV contest, how can she tell if this rugged, handsome older man is just being sweet for the cameras?

Love in the Darkness

A week in the dark has them seeing everything in a new light.

~

Please join the mailing list at

www.haleytravisromance.com

for new releases, updates, discounts & freebies!

~